W9-ATI-682

Carl Larsson

A FAMILY

With paintings by Carl Larsson
and a text by Lennart Rudström

G.P. Putnam's Sons New York

Carl Larsson the painter was born on May 28, 1853—a pale, cold little baby who seemed more dead than alive. But the midwife who brought him into the world gave him a sound slap on the bottom to make him cry and bring air into his lungs. He did cry, so all was well.

Carl grew up in the slums of Stockholm. He was often ill, lonely, and afraid, but he felt better if he could draw or look at pictures. He used to visit the seamstress next door so he could see the fashion plates she had pinned on the wall to cover the torn wallpaper. And he used to wait for his friend Corporal Ärtman to bring him pencil stubs and paper which the corporal stole from his regimental headquarters so Carl could draw.

Carl went to kindergarten at a free school for "poor children," where his teachers encouraged him to draw and paint. When he was thirteen, he entered the preparatory school of the Academy of Fine Arts.

Carl always knew he was going to be an artist, even when he was struggling to make a living. As it turned out, he became one of the finest artists in Sweden. After he was married, he especially enjoyed painting pictures of his family. So wasn't it lucky that he and his wife, Karin, had seven children? He was like a delighted father with a camera, snapping pictures whenever a scene struck his fancy.

Ulf and Pontus wearing helmets and armed with sabers—well, he couldn't let that pass! And little Brita balanced on his head! As he and Brita pranced about the room, he happened to glance in a mirror. What a picture! he thought. He grabbed paper and pencil and from a quick sketch came this painting. And, of course, he had to paint his Karin, standing with little Kersti who peeked shyly at her father.

In the nineteenth century there was so much poverty and distress in Sweden that many Swedes emigrated to America. When Carl Larsson was about ten years old, a terrible epidemic of cholera broke out in Stockholm. Carl remembered hearses rattling daily through the alleys of the poor district where he lived. One of his playmates, a little girl, died of cholera.

Later in his life, he tried to do everything in his power to give his own children a better environment in which to grow up. And in his pictures he wanted to show what a safe and cheerful childhood could mean.

In this quick sketch, Carl showed the scene of his birth as he imagined it.

ULF
PONTUS

C.L.
BRITA
1895

KARIN
KERSTI

The first model in the flock of children was Suzanne. When she was born, Carl wrote, "On August 11, Karin had a little girl—big and chubby! Now I am the happiest man in the world! I turn cartwheels and somersaults!"

Carl and Karin were living in the French village of Grez with other artists and writers from Europe and America when Suzanne was born. Nobody had much money, but never mind! Everyone shared as much as they could, just like a large family.

During the Christmas and New Year's holidays (1884–85), Carl Larsson painted "A Studio Idyll." Suzanne is resting in Karin's lap. Daylight enters through the studio window, shines on Karin's head, on her white lace collar, on the tip of her nose, and on Suzanne's forehead and face. Carl put the light there with his white pastel chalk.

At first the painting "Little Suzanne" was just a picture of a room, but Carl didn't like that at all. So he cut out a narrow strip where the chair was, then he put Suzanne on the chair with Karin bending over her. That was better!

When Suzanne was nine months old, the Larssons returned to Sweden. These two paintings were shown at art exhibits and were highly praised. They were the first of many paintings of the Larsson family.

Although Carl used many techniques, most of the pictures of his family that he painted later in life were done in watercolors. In "Studio Idyll," however, he used pastels, ordinary dry colored chalks, which he applied to grayish, pastel paper with a somewhat "fluffy" surface. He painted the darkest parts of Karin and Suzanne first and left the white reflections to the last. The painting "Little Suzanne" is done in oils.

The sketch you see here is of Corporal Ärtman, who brought Carl pencil stubs when Carl was a little boy.

Carl Larsson never grew tired of painting his family, but for a few years he did not do many portraits of the children, because he had to make enough money to live. So he illustrated books and worked as an art teacher—first in Stockholm (their apartment was small as a cupboard, Carl said), then in Gothenburg, then back in France.

In 1887 Carl's son Ulf was born. A year later, along came Pontus. But Carl had so many pupils! So many classes! And now he was working on sketches for a mural for the National Museum at Stockholm.

Sometimes he worried about not having enough time to spend with his family. Still, he did manage to do a few drawings of Pontus. The small black-and-white etching shown here was one he made as a New Year's greeting card.

The next year he made an oil painting "Pontus on the Floor." Pontus was sitting on a rag rug, playing with a doll and a wooden horse, when suddenly he turned around and looked at his father. It was a perfect pose, Carl thought. He made a sketch, then set up his canvas and easel and completed the painting.

Of course, Pontus didn't hold still all this time. The doll and the horse probably stayed where they were, but it is likely that Pontus got tired and fell asleep on the carpet.

"Pontus on the Floor" is painted in oils. Oil paints contain linseed oil, which dries slowly, so it usually takes much longer to finish an oil painting than a watercolor. Sometimes the painter has to wait several days for the underpainting to dry before he can continue with the other colors.

The picture of the newborn Pontus is an etching made after a drawing is completed. First, Carl drew the picture of Pontus onto a copper plate covered with beeswax and soot. After he treated the copper plate with acids, the drawing was engraved on it. Then when he put the plate into a printing machine, he could print as many "Pontus" pictures as he wanted.

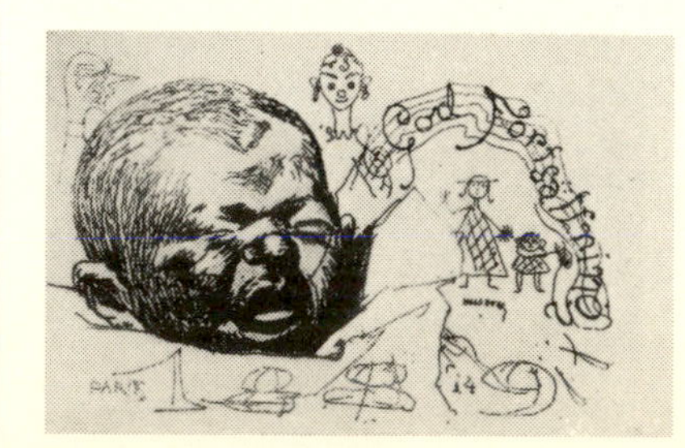

CALLE MÖLLER
FRU!

Once again the Larsson family had a new home. Karin's father gave them a cottage in Sundborn, in the province of Dalarna, and they began spending the summers there. Although it was small, there was a good studio for Carl and they added new rooms as the family grew. Now in addition to Suzanne, Ulf, and Pontus, there was Lisbeth.

While Carl worked hard at his painting and illustrating, Karin saw to the carpentry and painting for the new additions, did her weaving, and looked after this large family.

And what was a day like in Sundborn? "Goodness gracious," Carl wrote. "What a summer! The days disappear one after another and they are all alike. In the morning, one dives into the lake, one eats one's porridge, and takes a look at every flower and every leaf on the property to find out if they have grown during the night. And then one takes one's easel and things and sets out . . ."

Dinner came at half-past one; after that, Carl would work on illustrations for books until five o'clock. When the illustrating time was over, Carl would have a snack—a quick cup of coffee with buns. Then away he'd go with his painting materials on his shoulder, while Karin carried the picnic hamper. He worked until dark, which was very late, since this was summer, when the sun hardly sets at all in Sweden. The last job of the day was to herd the ducks and hens into the shed.

In May 1893, a fifth child was born. Little Brita. Carl and Karin were spending a vacation in a fisherman's cottage on the west coast of Sweden when Brita arrived. Here is Karin nursing the two-week-old baby.

The illustration of a book is not quickly done. Carl Larsson complained about the fact that the work on "Songs and Ditties" by Elias Sehlstedt took so much time—a couple of years. Still, he thought that it was an unusually pleasant job. *"If I can get my works of art distributed in this way round the world, I'll not bother about painting pictures,"* he said. But, of course, he did bother. He was always challenged by new ideas, whether it was a picture for a small greeting card or one for a large mural.

This lively cow is a sketch for one of the verses in "Songs and Ditties."

But Carl was doing what he liked best now; he was painting the children. When a writer named Henriques happened to see a painting of ten-year-old Suzanne, he liked it so much, he ordered one for himself. Then a man in Gothenburg saw that painting, and he liked it so much, he ordered a painting of each of the children in the Larsson family. But as new children kept coming, Carl was told: "Though maybe you can afford to have so many children, I can't afford to pay for so many portraits."

Here is Lisbeth wearing red stockings, a red dress, a red apron, and carrying her red doll. "Lisbeth, the little rascal," Carl wrote, "is like a little troll sparkling in the sunshine. There is brightness and glitter around her, and bubbling and tinkling laughter. There is giggling, and there is no sorrow wherever she goes."

That same year Carl painted a serious painting of Suzanne, wearing her best dress and standing on a stool. She seems solemn, but after all, she's been standing a long time. And it is tiring—always having to be a model!

The children often served as models for their father. Usually they dressed in their own clothes, but sometimes they dressed in historical costumes. Carl's large paintings and murals with historical themes were usually done for museums, schools, and theaters.

There was a shed at their home in Sundborn filled with costumes which Karin had designed and sewn. You can be sure that the children used them to dress up for play and for masquerade parties.

LISBETH

SUZANNE

In the summer of 1894 it rained for six weeks without stopping. Carl was restless and unhappy because he could not go outside and paint. Karin suggested that he paint scenes inside their home, and he did. Someone in the family appears in nearly every painting.

That autumn they were shown in a large exhibition in Stockholm, and they received so much praise that they were eventually published five years later in a book called *A Home*. The book had paintings of the family indoors and outdoors, with Carl's own words describing life at Sundborn.

One of the paintings was of Lisbeth at the rowboat harbor, staring into the water. The Sundborn river is like a mirror with the birches reflected in it. The clouds are flimsy and light and the air is still.

Lisbeth doesn't move a muscle because she is waiting for an old pike, or at least a perch that is bigger than the one Ulf and Pontus caught when they were out in their rowboat.

Just by looking at Lisbeth's back, one can almost tell what is on her mind. She can see the fisherman in his boat out on the river and perhaps she is wondering, "What if he catches that old pike before I do!"

The series of paintings from the Larsson home in Sundborn became well known in many parts of the world. They convey the feeling of an ideal home where everything is beautiful and free from worry.

Indeed, the life represented in these pictures seemed so serene and gay that many soldiers in the First World War took Carl Larsson's books to the front with them.

Although the paintings that Carl created of his home and family look so happy, there was also sorrow at Sundborn, just as there is sometimes sadness in every home. Carl himself was not always happy, as he has shown in portraits of himself. Here you see him as "the writer's ghost."

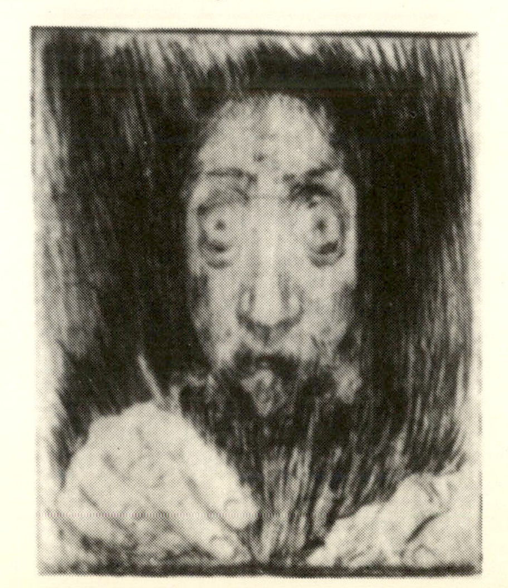

Carl Larsson had always wanted to own a farm. In 1897, he bought two, *Spadarvet,* five minutes walk from the family home, and *Kartbacken,* which was also nearby.

Johan and Johanna who worked at *Spadarvet* stayed on and ran the farm, and Carl's parents, who were now old, went to live at *Kartbacken.*

And little Kersti was added to the family.

Here is Brita a few years later, standing on the path at *Spadarvet.* And how did she get into the picture? Perhaps she had been in the kitchen to get a piece of bread and raspberry jam from Johanna—and a little something for the cat. On her way out, there was Carl with his painting equipment. Brita was caught!

She had to stand with the bread and jam in her hand while Carl did a pencil sketch, put in the outline with India ink, dipped his paintbrush in the water jar, and laid on the first colors—red and green and yellow and blue.

Later on when he painted grass and leaves and flowers, she could, of course, leave. Maybe she went right back into the kitchen for more bread and jam. Maybe the cat went too.

The year the Larssons bought the farm, was a hard one for Carl. He was completing his mural paintings for the National Museum in Stockholm.

An Italian helper arrived at four o'clock each morning to plaster a small section of the large wall surface on which he was working. Carl started painting at six or seven o'clock and continued on and on, no matter how tired he was. If by evening he had not finished painting the freshly plastered surface, everything had to be chipped away and a new start had to be made. An artist has to work quickly on plaster before it dries or it is no good

But don't think for a moment that the Larssons had stopped moving! They had spent ten summers at the house in Sundborn, and in 1900 they went there to live for good. They built new rooms and a bigger studio for Carl.

And guess what else was new in the family! Yes, another baby, little Esbjörn is on Karin's lap. Carl painted him quickly with lots of water in the paint so that he'd look just as delicate and pink as a baby really does look.

In the other picture, the family have just finished their supper. The children are half-hidden as the objects on the table become the center of Carl's attention: a platter of ham, a mustard pot, a sugar bowl, jugs, mugs, empty plates, napkins, a vase of flowers, and an oil lamp casting its light over all.

There is a real feeling of evening in the scene, with tired but satisfied children who cannot eat another bite. In the shadows Karin is standing with little Esbjörn in her arms; they have just come in to say good night.

At the same time that Carl was painting his family, he continued with his historical works. Now that they lived permanently at Sundborn and Carl had a larger studio, he did most of this painting at home.

One of his best-known historical paintings is "Gustavus Vasa's Entry Into Stockholm." He did his first color sketch for this work as early as 1891, but the final painting was not completed until sixteen years later.

Lisbeth served as the model for the flower girl who is going to crown the king with a wreath.

C.L.
SUNDBORN
1900
ESBJÖRN
NOV. 1900 I SVNDBORN

The same table, the same dining room, the same oil lamp. But this is a different evening, a year later. A gloomy winter evening with a storm raging outside.

"It is terrible outdoors," Carl wrote. "The wind is whistling at the corners of the house, and the snow isn't snow, it is needles stabbing your eyes. And while you are crying, hobgoblins are whipping your back with canes. Oh, to get indoors and play a game of cards!"

Inside it is warm and cozy. Carl must be just out of sight, sketching, for Brita and Kersti and Karin are all looking at him. Perhaps they are saying, "Oh, do hurry," for guests are obviously expected. There is a bowl of apples, pears, and grapes on the table. Teacups and a teapot and tray with four glasses are set out. Karin takes down a bottle of Benedictine to put on the tray. And through the open door, one can see candles on the table where the grown-ups will play cards.

Carl liked to paint different sayings over the doorways throughout the house. Over the door in this painting are the words, "The Peace of the Lord." Over the door to the entry he painted a portrait of Esbjörn and the words, "I tell you; be happy as a child." And over another door he wrote, "Love each other children, for love is everything."

It is not only Carl Larsson's large murals that are to be found in Swedish museums. Almost all the pictures in this book are borrowed from museum collections.

This oil painting of the Larssons in their dining room ended up in the National Museum in Stockholm. There it is now for all of us to see what it was like that cold winter night in 1901 when the Larssons were getting ready for company.

The sketch of Karin combing her daughter's hair is in the Gothenburg Museum.

Guds Fred
C.L.
1901

Here is Suzanne, standing on a chair with a paintbrush in her hand, working on a design of flowers, leaves, and garlands. Carl wanted to catch the exact moment when Suzanne stopped to study her work. Other painters can be seen through the windows—one on a scaffolding, another on a ladder.

But look at the shadows and light—how the light from the far window shines on Suzanne's braid and on the folds of her apron! And all the colors! The blue tones on her blouse and apron, on the chair and walls, and the red and green and yellow in the border around the wall. The whole room smells of fresh paint and summer.

And here is Carl's father coming up the path, almost hidden by sunflowers, bleeding hearts, and blueweed. He is bent and old and finds walking difficult. And he is lonely. Carl and his father never quite understood each other, and though Carl was sorry for him, it was too late for them to become real friends. Perhaps that is why Carl painted his father so small and far away.

Both of these pictures—the one of Suzanne painting and the one of Carl's father—are bright with color and light. Perhaps Carl was trying to make up for the drabness of his own childhood, which he never forgot. This is what he himself had to say about it: "*. . . One room and kitchen, with big holes in the walls, and these holes full of cockroaches, armies of them, and other vermin. One can hardly say that things looked promising. Mother sobbed and Father prowled around, gloomy and embarrassed.*"

Perhaps this is another reason why Carl took such pleasure in sketching and painting his own children.

In 1903 Carl was asked to make a large painting for the assembly hall in a school at Gothenburg. What would the subject be? At first Carl didn't know what he wanted to paint. Finally, after a restless night of thinking, he came up with an idea. St. George and the Dragon! The famous story of England's patron saint.

He started to work on sketches, and Karin began sewing the costumes for the models to wear. And then something happened to change Carl's mind. It was a sunny day in early summer, and suddenly he caught sight of a long line of children walking past the house, carrying wreaths and bouquets of flowers. This was the last day of school, and the children were going to decorate the schoolhouse for closing ceremonies.

There was his picture! Carl thought. Why bother with St. George and the Dragon? These models would not need such elaborate costumes. All he had to do was to gather his own children and their friends together.

Lisbeth would have a wreath of flowers; Brita would walk beside Lisbeth and carry a bouquet of blue cornflowers. The others would follow in a line: a sailor boy with a wheelbarrow full of birch branches, some girls with buckets and brushes, others with bunches of lilacs, a boy with spruce twigs, a little girl with meadow flowers.

On their way the children would meet a wandering beggar, a soldier on horseback, and a woman in mourning. "There will be a lot to think about in this picture," Carl said.

Carl called it "Outside the Summer Winds Are Blowing," and it is pictured on the front of the book. The original painting was hung in the school in 1903, and there it still hangs, bright as a June day.

As early as 1886, Carl worked on the St. George and the Dragon theme to be used on a catalog for an exhibition.

Carl had to make many detailed drawings for "Outside Summer Winds Are Blowing," like the one of the girl with the pail and the scrubbing brush, which he did in charcoal and chalk.

That same year Carl painted a watercolor called "Mother and Daughter." Karin is sitting in a striped apron, her hands resting in her lap, while Suzanne, as a young woman, stands in the middle of the floor. The two seem to be on a stage in the middle of a performance, talking about serious matters. But it is a performance without words. Nobody knows what they are saying.

Perhaps Carl spoke to them like a stage director: "Turn your head a little to the right. Drop your eyes so that you look tired and sad. And Suzanne, step back a pace. The distance between you and Karin must be greater. There must be a feeling that you are talking about something serious, that something has happened which cannot be solved at the moment."

Though Carl Larsson might be serious sometimes, he was just as often amusing. Sometimes he drew entire series of the children and their antics, as you can see in these extracts from his family album.

In 1905 Carl and Karin's oldest son Ulf died. These were sad years, but Carl's painting in this period became more luminous than ever, as if he were trying to bring light to his sorrow.

"Karin on the Shore," painted in 1908, is just such a picture. There is Karin, walking along the shore, far away in thought. Everything is still—the river smooth as glass, the girl with her dog in the boat, rowing, oh, so slowly. But have you ever seen such clear, sparkling water? Such brilliant red flowers? Such a peaceful summer day? The light appears especially bright in contrast to the black dress that Karin is wearing. And Karin's face and hands seem to draw their warm red color from the red flowers and the red path. One would like to tell Karin to look up and see what a glorious day it is.

Carl Larsson often tells a whole story in a single black-and-white drawing without using any color at all. Look at this drawing of Esbjörn with the mumps. There he is, swollen and muffled up, but he is not too ill. Indeed, he seems quite proud to be serving as a model. Imagine an artist being able to say so much with a pencil and an ordinary sheet of paper!

C.L.
1908

Now it is 1918 and here is Esbjörn, the youngest one in the family, sitting on the porch, reading. He is eighteen-years-old; the next year he would graduate from school. "And after that," Carl said, "he is going to be a farmer as his ancestors were."

Carl was feeling tired and ill these days. He found it more and more difficult to paint. Perhaps when he came out on the porch, he didn't intend to paint at all. Perhaps he was simply going to have a chat with Esbjörn. Perhaps he sat down on the opposite bench. But seeing Esbjörn, a cushion behind his back, his feet on the railing, a book on his knee, Carl changed his mind. Besides it was a wonderful day, pleasantly warm, pleasantly breezy, with a bumblebee buzzing among the flowers. Carl got up and went indoors for his watercolor paper, pencil, and paints.

Was Carl Larsson content to paint these small paintings of his family and surroundings? "No, of course I'm not," he once wrote. "I dream of walls as big as Ladugårdslandet and I hope to get them beyond the grave . . ." Yet it is these simple paintings of his home and family, which he could never resist painting, for which he is best remembered and loved.

Not only the members of the family served as models, but many people in the village as well. And Carl had a photograph taken of himself on horseback in order to be able to use it as a model when he painted Gustavus Vasa riding over the bridge into Stockholm.

Sometimes one can pick out the children and the grandfather and the joiner and the bricklayer and the painter in his books. They may be disguised as knights or kings or infantrymen, but never mind—we know they are all Carl Larsson's friends.

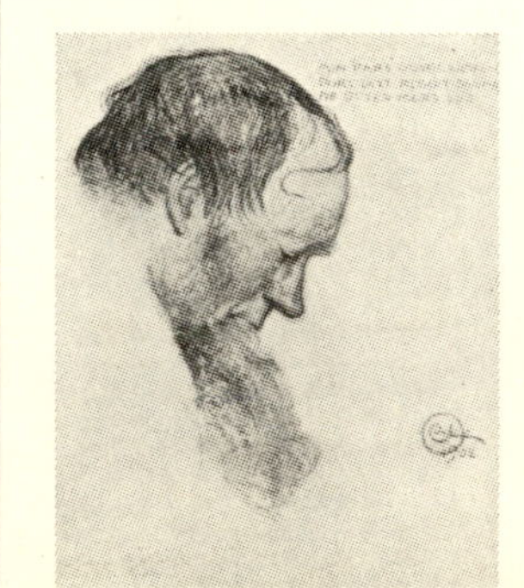

As it turned out, the portrait of Esbjörn on the porch was one of Carl's last paintings. Carl Larsson died in January 1919, at the age of sixty-six. But wasn't it fortunate that he had shared his family with the world? No matter how many years pass, one can drop in on his family and catch the children, just as Carl did, right in the middle of whatever they are doing.

Step back, for instance, to Christmas Eve in 1892. One feels, just as in all Carl Larsson's paintings, as if one had walked into a story. What is going to happen next? What does Ulf see through the keyhole? What does Suzanne hear? Pontus wants to know, too, while little Lisbeth just smiles. Perhaps she does not know yet what Christmas is, but she will soon find out. Perhaps she is just smiling at Carl who has his pencil and paper and has caught them again.

Beneath this picture Carl wrote: "Memories of the kids at Sundborn."

So many happy memories!

In the series of drawings shown here, Carl Larsson described some of the events in his life. The drawings were made to go with these verses which Carl wrote:

Out in the street, I kissed all
the girls in sight,
I somehow seemed to think
it was my right.
As for the boys, I simply
boxed their ears,
And they ran home to
mother, shedding tears.

I had to saw the firewood
trim and neat,
But seldom got a crust of
bread to eat.
I carried water for the
women old,
And made at that a tidy
heap of gold.

Our teacher shouted threats
into my ear,
And pounded with a cane
my tender rear.
But when he saw my
drawings, he cried out,
"Why, you're a genius, lad,
and not a lout!"

TILL EMMY
ETT MINNE AF
UNGARNA I SUNDBORN

Published simultaneously in Canada by Longman Canada Limited, Toronto.
Printed in Portugal by Gris Impressores 1979.

LIBRARY OF CONGRESS CATALOGING IN PUBLICATION DATA
Larsson, Carl Olof, 1853–1919.
A family.
Translation of En malare och hans familj.
SUMMARY: Reproductions of several of Larsson's paintings of his large family are accompanied by commentary on the paintings, the life, and the career of this noted Swedish artist.
1. Larsson, Carl Olof, 1853–1919—Juvenile literature.
2. Painters—Sweden—Biography—Juvenile literature.
[1. Larsson, Carl Olof, 1853–1919. 2. Artists. 3. Sweden—Social life and customs] I. Rudström, Lennart. II. Title.
ND793.L27A4 1979 759.85 [B] 79-14291
ISBN 0-399-20700-7

BIBLIOGRAPHY

The following books have been used as sources for this book:

De Mina Och Annat Gammalt Krafs (Carl Larsson)
Ett hem (Carl Larsson)
Spadarvet (Carl Larsson)
Jag—En Bok Om Och På Både Gott Och Ont Av Carl Larsson (Carl Larsson)
Carl Larsson Skildrad Av Honom Själv (An historical anthology by Harriet and Sven Alfons)
Carl Larsson (Georg Nordensvan)
Carl Larsson Som Etsare (Axel L. Romdahl)

Quotations in *A Family* are taken from these sources.

The following institutions have contributed picture materials:

Art Museum of Gothenberg: 3, 5, (right), 6, 11, 17 (right), 18, 26, back cover.
Hvitfeldtska läroverket in Gothenberg: cover, p.23.
Malmö Museum: p.14, 27.
National Museum in Stockholm: p.5 (left), 7, 13, 16, 19, 21 (right), 22.
Thielska Gallery in Stockholm: p 17 (left), 25.
Waldemarsudde in Stockholm: p.9.
Carl Larsson's home, Sundborn: p. 31.
In private possession: p.1, 15, 21 (left), 29.